For the 141 tribe, your fingerprints
are all over everything. Love you—M. F.

For Isabel and Jay—D. S.

BEACH LANE BOOKS
An imprint of Simon & Schuster Children's Publishing Division
1230 Avenue of the Americas, New York, New York 10020
Text copyright © 2018 by Meg Fleming • Illustrations copyright © 2018 by Diana Sudyka
All rights reserved, including the right of reproduction in whole or in part in any form.
BEACH LANE BOOKS is a trademark of Simon & Schuster, Inc.
For information about special discounts for bulk purchases, please contact
Simon & Schuster Special Sales at 1-866-506-1949 or business@simonandschuster.com.
The Simon & Schuster Speakers Bureau can bring authors to your live event.
For more information or to book an event, contact the Simon & Schuster Speakers Bureau at 1-866-248-3049 or
visit our website at www.simonspeakers.com.
Book design by Lauren Rille • The text for this book was set in Belucian.
The illustrations for this book were rendered in gouache watercolor.
Manufactured in China • 0818 SCP • First Edition • 10 9 8 7 6 5 4 3 2 1
Library of Congress Cataloging-in-Publication Data
Names: Fleming, Meg, author. | Sudyka, Diana, illustrator. • Title: Sometimes rain / Meg Fleming ; illustrated by Diana Sudyka.
Description: First edition. | New York : Beach Lane Books, [2018] | Summary: Illustrations and simple,
rhyming text celebrate the seasons of the year and the joy each one brings. • Identifiers: LCCN 2017038883
ISBN 9781481459181 (hardcover) | ISBN 9781481459198 (eBook) • Subjects: | CYAC: Stories in rhyme. • Seasons—Fiction.
Classification: LCC PZ8.3.F639 Som 2018 | DDC [E]—dc23 LC record available at https://lccn.loc.gov/2017038883)

Sometimes Rain

WORDS BY
Meg Fleming

ILLUSTRATIONS BY
Diana Sudyka

Beach Lane Books • New York London Toronto Sydney New Delhi

Sometimes drizzle.
Drip-drip drain.

Sometimes picnic.
Sometimes rain.

Sometimes dropping.
Steady chill.

Sometimes frosting every hill.

Sometimes sledding.
Frozen toes.

Sometimes
carrot.

Sometimes nose.

Sometimes twinkle.
Winter white.

Crystal garden.
Silver night.

Sometimes boring.
Wonder, wait.

Sometimes early.

Sometimes late.

Sometimes clear.
Bright and glowing.

So much melt,
the mud is growing!

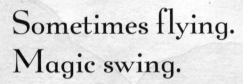

Sometimes flying.
Magic swing.

Blooming treehouse.
Happy spring.

Sometimes dreaming.
Open skies.

Sometimes chasing butterflies.

Sometimes blazing secret trails.

Sometimes finding
frogs and snails.

Sometimes splashing.
Yellow sun.

Sometimes soaking summer fun.

Sometimes changing.
Vibrant trees.

Sometimes zipping-out
the breeze.

Sometimes stomping.
Leafy crunch.

Sometimes eating apple-lunch.

Sometimes piles.
Ten feet tall.

Sometimes jumping
into fall.

Sometimes wandering.
Far or near.

Always knowing someone here.

Always ready.
Stay or roam.

Always welcome . . .

always home.

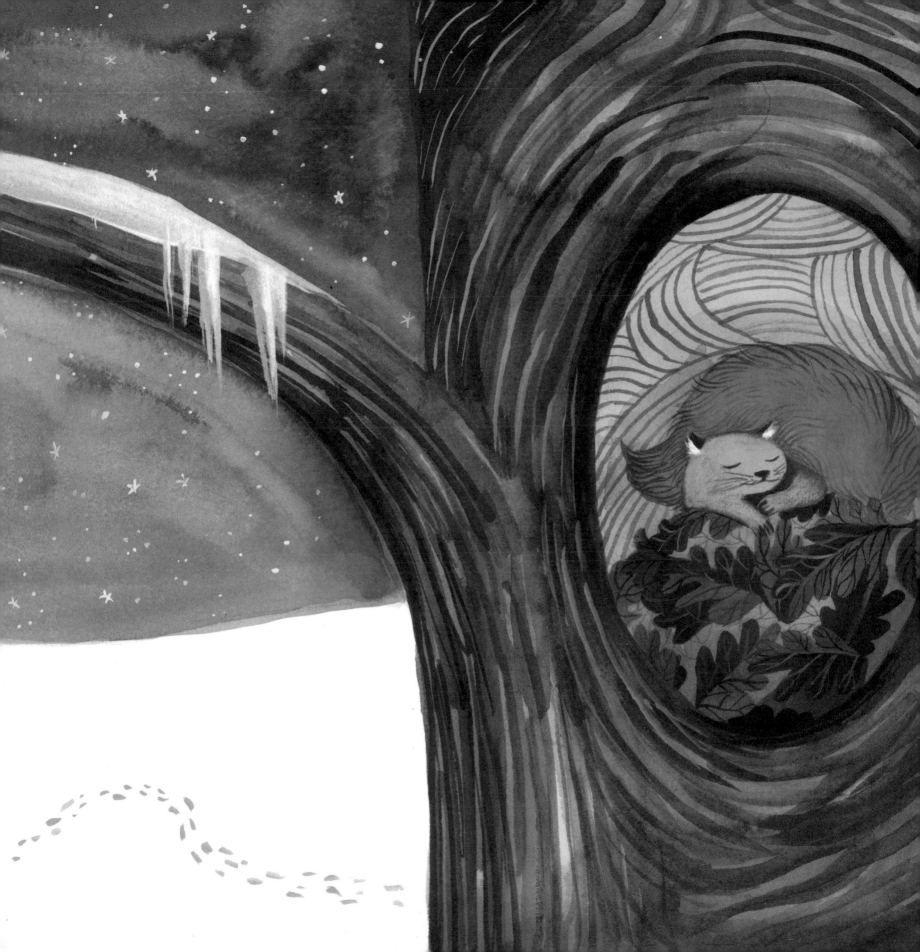